Leo.W

Leo.W

WHERE DO THEY GO?

PART ONE

B.D DONALDSON

Where Do They Go?
Copyright 2016 Barry Donaldson

Wholesale discounts for book orders are
available through Ingram Distributors.

Tellwell Talent
www.tellwell.ca

ISBN
Paperback: 978-1-77302-243-7
Hardcover: 978-1-77302-244-4

"There are moments when you miss someone so much, you wish you could just pick them out of your dreams and hug them."

Love you Mom.

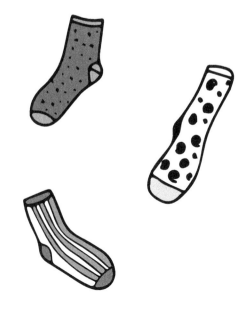

Mrs. Williams looked into the washing machine and took out four pairs of socks. At the very bottom she found just one last black sock all by itself. *Where was the other one?* she wondered.

"Jaylen, where is your other sock?" Mrs. Williams asked as she went up the stairs.

Naleaha and Jaylen did not answer, but Mrs. Williams could hear them giggling.

Mrs. Williams entered the children's bedroom holding Jaylen's lone sock in her hand.

"Where is the other one?" she asked him.

"I don't know, Mom. I wore it home from school yesterday."

"Well, you'd better find it, or I will take away your video games," she said.

Right before bedtime Jaylen looked at Naleaha and asked, "Where could my sock be?"

"I don't know. Maybe there is a monster that eats socks," she said.

Later that night as the children were sleeping, their dog
Max heard a sound. He got up and began to bark. The
sound was coming from the other side of the bedroom door.

Max's barking woke up Naleaha and Jaylen.

"What is it, Max?" Naleaha asked.

Naleaha and Jaylen saw a shadow under the door.

The children jumped out of their beds and quickly opened the door. But there was no one there.

In the morning as Jaylen got dressed for school, he could only find one of his favourite grey socks.

"Have you seen my other sock, Naleaha?"
he asked his sister.

"No, a monster took it," laughed Naleaha.

When the children came home from school that afternoon, Jaylen rushed into the house to look for his missing favourite grey sock.

He did not want his mother to punish him for losing another sock.

At bedtime, Naleaha had an idea of how to help Jaylen find his sock. "Let's put a camera on Max so he can record anything that happens while we are sleeping," she said.

"Okay," said Jaylen. But he did not believe in monsters.

Before they fell asleep, Naleaha and Jaylen made sure the camera was working.

"Now we'll finally find out who is taking away our socks," Naleaha said.

The children woke up early the next morning and attached the camera to the computer. They looked at the video but didn't see anything out of the ordinary.

"We will never find out who is taking away our socks," Jaylen said sadly.

The next morning Naleaha decided to check the
camera again.

"Jaylen, come quick!" she yelled.

"What is it?" he asked, slowly getting out of bed.

"It looks like something from outer space,"
she said excitedly.

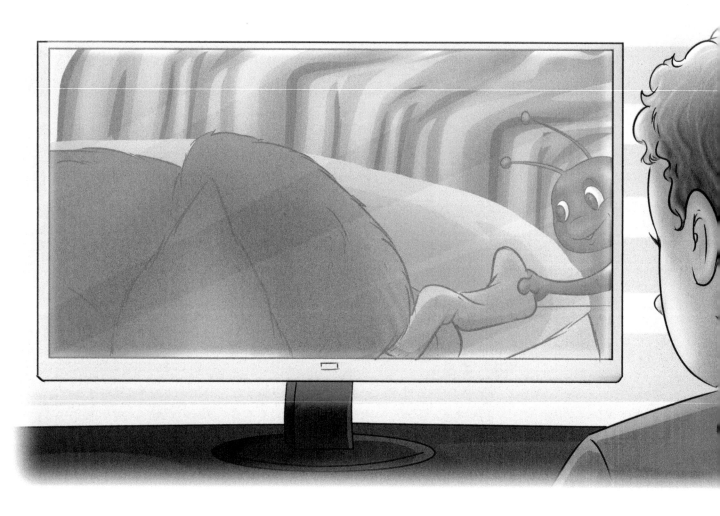

The camera showed a little alien creeping up to Max while the dog was sleeping and grabbing one of Jaylen's black socks right from under his paw.

"What did I tell you?" Naleaha asked her brother.

"Well, it is not a monster," he said.

"But it is an alien. How are we going to catch him now?" Naleaha replied.

They thought of many ideas.

First, they made a trap using a stick to hold up a basket.
Then they put a sock under the basket to use as bait.
When the alien tried to get the sock, the basket would fall
down on him.

The next morning the trap had fallen down and the sock
was gone. But the alien was not underneath the basket.

The next night Naleaha tried to stay awake for as long as she could. Just as she was about to fall asleep, she heard a strange little sound. She listened and looked over at the computer. There was the alien, sitting in front of the computer.

The alien was busy removing the pictures of himself that the children had downloaded from the camera to the computer. He had no idea that Naleaha had woken up and was watching him.

Meanwhile, Naleaha quietly got out of bed and slowly crept toward the alien.

The alien saw her reflection on the computer screen.

The alien turned around in the chair and simply stared at Naleaha. At first, he was too frightened to speak. Just as he opened his mouth, Naleaha began to scream.

Her scream woke up Jaylen. The three of them stared and stared at each other, they were so surprised.

Jaylen could not believe what he was seeing.

Suddenly, the alien jumped down off of the chair and began hopping over toward the closet door.

Naleaha shouted, "Stop! Where are you going? Where do you come from?"

But the alien did not stop. He kept hopping away.

While they were watching, the alien ran into the closet and slammed the door behind him. Jaylen looked down and noticed a sock was missing from his foot.

"Mom is never going to believe this," he said.

The children ran after the alien. They couldn't believe their eyes.

"Hurry, he has my sock," Jaylen said.

The children opened the closet door, but the alien was gone.

"Where did he go?" Jaylen asked.

"I don't know," said Naleaha. "But I'm sure he will come back."

TO BE CONTINUED...

CPSIA information can be obtained
at www.ICGtesting.com
Printed in the USA
LVOW05s2305101116
512017LV00007B/8/P